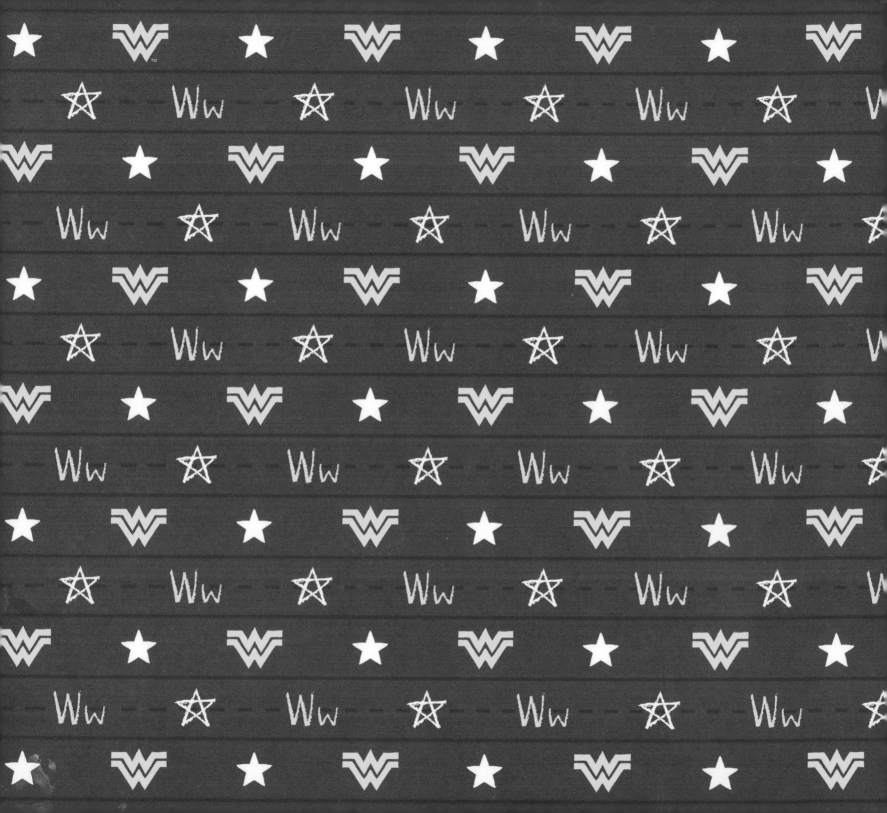

Be a Star, Wonder Woman! is published by
Capstone Young Readers
a Capstone imprint
1710 Roe Crest Drive
North Mankato, Minnesota 56003
www.mycapstone.com

STAR38959

Cataloging-in-Publication Data is available on the
Library of Congress website.

ISBN: 978-1-62370-875-7 (jacketed hardcover)

Jacket and book design by Bob Lentz

Printed and bound in the USA.
010352F17

words by Michael Dahl

pictures by Omar Lozano

BE A STAR,

WONDER WOMAN!

Wonder Woman created by
William Moulton Marston

CAPSTONE YOUNG READERS
a Capstone imprint

New challenges await.

. . . one hero
shines bright.

She is prepared.
She is ready . . . .

Let go!

To restore peace . . .

For no matter how tough the challenge . . .

. . . or how difficult the task . . .

Be a star, Wonder Woman!

Be a STAR Checklist!

1.

Be Prepared

2.

Be Kind

3.

Be Brave

4.

Be Honest

5.

Be Strong

6.

Be Heroic

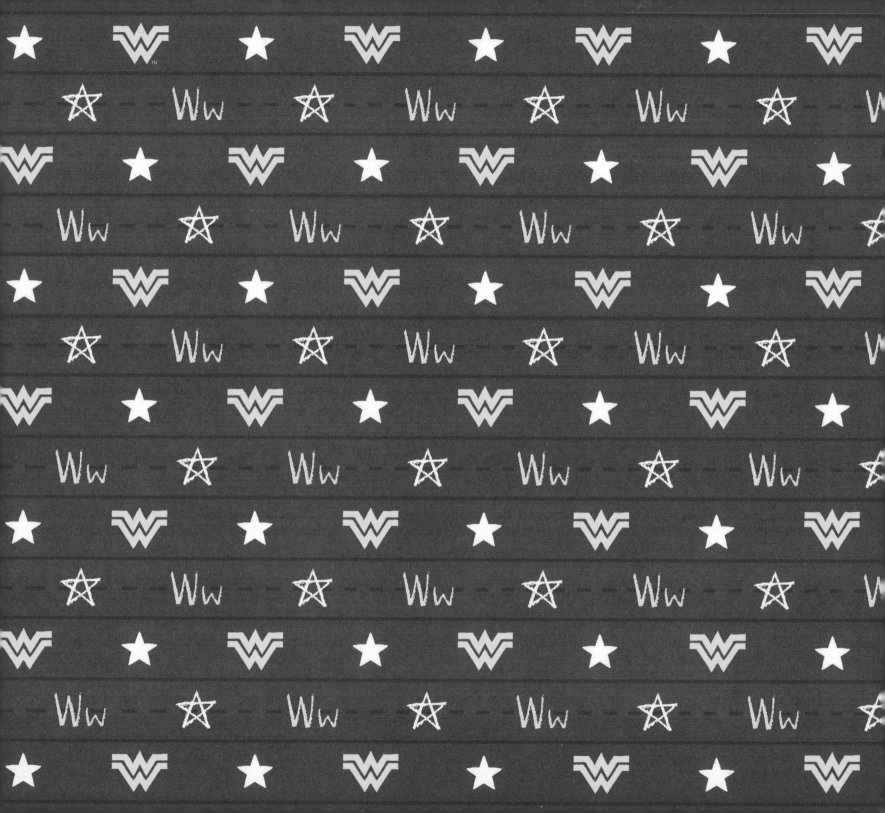